To Elizabeth, with love R.E.
To Pearl C.F.

OXFORD
UNIVERSITY PRESS

Great Clarendon Street, Oxford OX2 6DP

Oxford University Press is a department of the University of Oxford.
It furthers the University's objective of excellence in research, scholarship,
and education by publishing worldwide in

Oxford New York
Auckland Cape Town Dar es Salaam Hong Kong Karachi
Kuala Lumpur Madrid Melbourne Mexico City Nairobi
New Delhi Shanghai Taipei Toronto

With offices in
Argentina Austria Brazil Chile Czech Republic France Greece
Guatemala Hungary Italy Japan Poland Portugal Singapore
South Korea Switzerland Thailand Turkey Ukraine Vietnam

Oxford is a registered trade mark of Oxford University Press
in the UK and in certain other countries

Text © Richard Edwards 2005
Illustrations © Chris Fisher 2005
The moral rights of the author and artist have been asserted
Database right Oxford University Press (maker)

First published in 2005

British Library Cataloguing in Publication Data available

ISBN–13: 978–0-19-911254-8 Hardback
ISBN–10: 0-19-911254-1 Hardback

ISBN–13: 978–0-19-911129-9 Paperback
ISBN–10: 0-19-911129-4 Paperback

1 3 5 7 9 10 8 6 4 2
Printed in China

Nonsense
ABC
Rhymes

Written by Richard Edwards
Illustrated by Chris Fisher

OXFORD
UNIVERSITY PRESS

A

What does A stand for?

'Air,' says the balloon,

'Auntie,' says Uncle,

'Astronaut,' says the moon,

The magician says 'Abracadabra,'

'Africa,' says the gnu,

'Autumn,' says the falling leaf,

The sneeze says 'A-Atchoo!'

B

What does B stand for?
'Bristles,' says the broom,
'Bricks,' says the builder,
The thunder says 'Boom!'
'Bamboo,' says the panda,
'Baa!' says the sheep,
'Big,' says the elephant,
The car says 'Beep!'

C

What does C stand for?
'Cheese,' say the mice,
'Christmas,' says Santa Claus,
'Curry,' says the rice,
The rabbit says 'Carrot,'
The crow says 'Caw!'
The teddy says 'Cuddle me,'
'Creak,' says the floor.

Caw!

D

What does D stand for?
'Digging,' says the spade,
The hoover says 'Dust',
'Darkness,' says the shade,
'Dive,' says the dolphin,
'Drip,' says the rain,
Red says 'Danger,'
'Dribble,' says the drain.

DANGER!

E

What does E stand for?
The telescope says 'Eye,'
'Earth,' says the earthworm,
'Eat me!' says the pie,
'Exams,' says the teacher,
The donkey says 'Eeyore!'
'Echo,' says the echo,
'Enter,' says the door.

Exams!

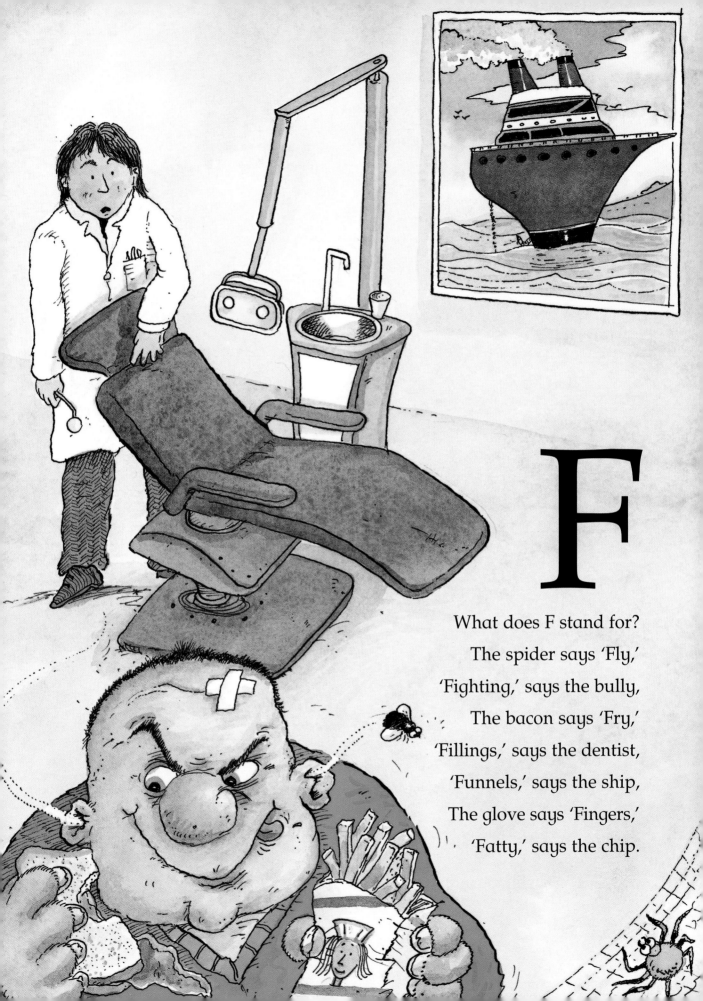

F

What does F stand for?
The spider says 'Fly,'
'Fighting,' says the bully,
The bacon says 'Fry,'
'Fillings,' says the dentist,
'Funnels,' says the ship,
The glove says 'Fingers,'
'Fatty,' says the chip.

G

What does G stand for?
'Green,' says the grass,
Granny says 'Grandad,'
The bottle says 'Glass,'
The turkey says 'Gobble,'
'Gloo-oo-my,' says the owl,
'Gurgle,' says the plughole,
The tiger says 'Growl!'

H

What does H stand for?
'Hay,' says the horse,
The teacher says 'Homework,'
The sun says 'Hot,' (of course),
'Herring,' says the fisherman,
The barber says 'Hair,'
The farmer says 'Harvest,'
'Honey,' says the bear.

I

What does I stand for?
'Ice,' says the rink,
'Itsy-bitsy,' says the ant,
The pen says 'Ink,'
'Igloo,' says the Eskimo,
'Itchy,' says the flea,
'Ill,' says the doctor,
'I,' says me.

J

What does J stand for?
'Jingle,' says the bell,
'Juice,' says the orange,
The jug says 'Juice' as well,
'Jungle,' says the jaguar,
'Jam,' says the jar,
The kangaroo says 'Jumping,'
'Journey,' says the car.

K

What does K stand for?
The Queen says 'King,'
The football says 'Kick me,'
'Knot,' says the string,
The burger says 'Ketchup,'
The lock says 'Key,'
The pot says 'Kettle,'
'Knobbly,' says the knee.

L

What does L stand for?

'Lolly,' says the stick,

'Ladder,' says the window cleaner,

The tongue says 'Lick,'

'Letters,' says the postman,

'Long,' says the giraffe,

The slug says 'Lettuces,'

The clown says 'Laugh'.

M

What does M stand for?
The kitten says 'Miaow,'
The toast says 'Marmalade,'
'Moo,' says the cow,
'Money,' says the banker,
'Mountain,' says the ski,
'Mouse,' says the computer,
'Mug,' says the tea.

Miaow!

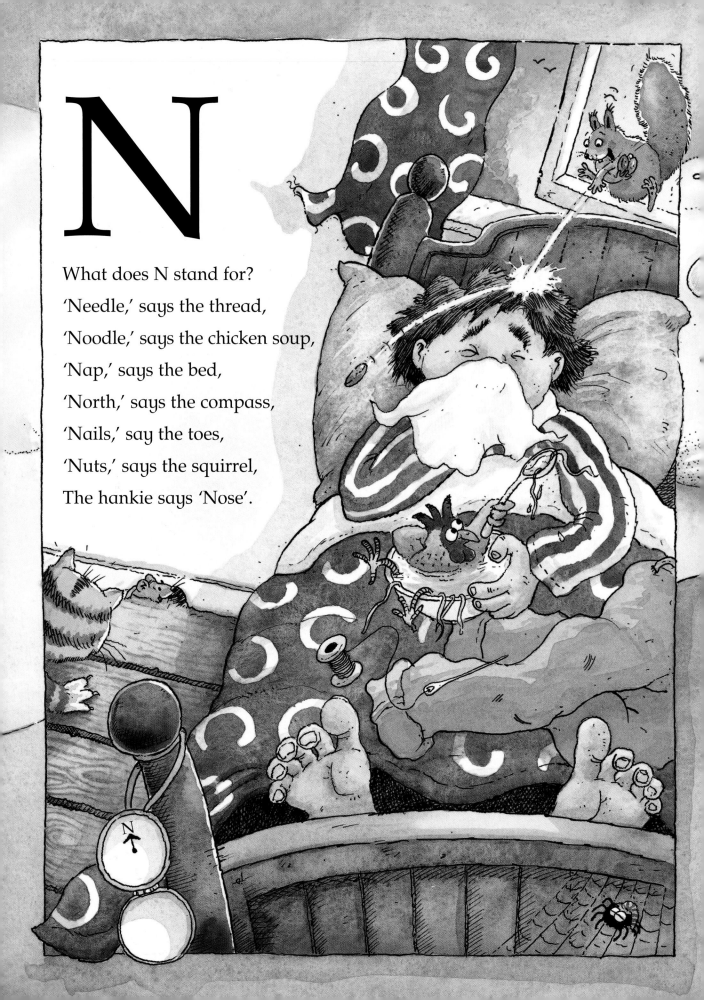

N

What does N stand for?

'Needle,' says the thread,

'Noodle,' says the chicken soup,

'Nap,' says the bed,

'North,' says the compass,

'Nails,' say the toes,

'Nuts,' says the squirrel,

The hankie says 'Nose'.

O

What does O stand for?
'Oven,' says the stew,
'Oasis,' says the camel,
The ghost says 'Ooooo!'
The shop says 'Open,'
'Orchard,' says the tree,
'Ocean, Ocean, Ocean,'
Says the whale in the sea.

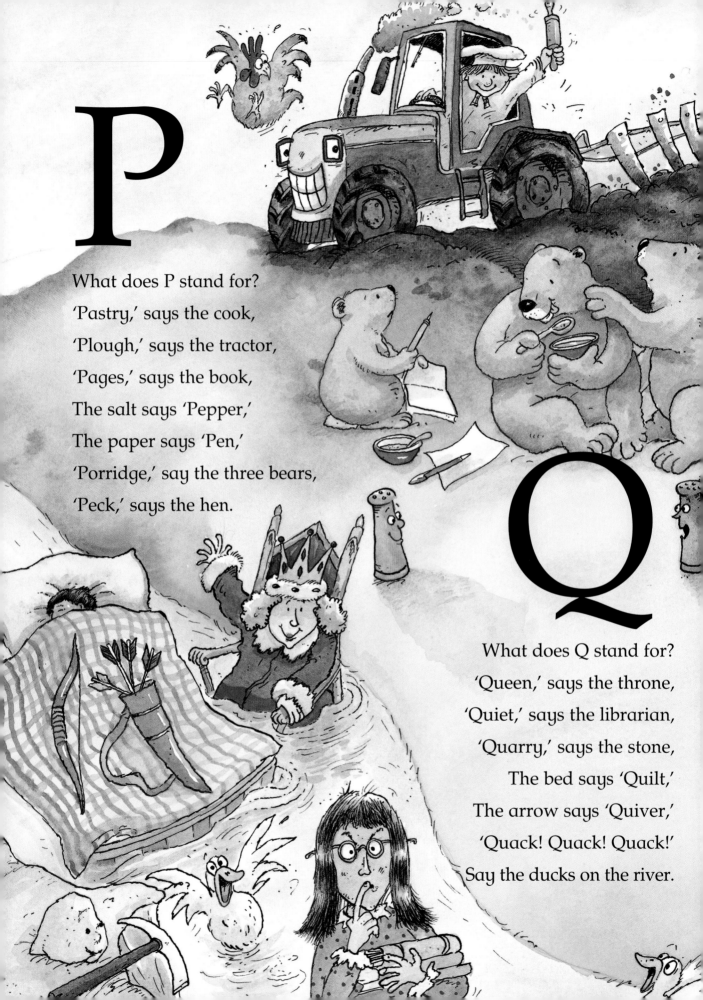

P

What does P stand for?
'Pastry,' says the cook,
'Plough,' says the tractor,
'Pages,' says the book,
The salt says 'Pepper,'
The paper says 'Pen,'
'Porridge,' say the three bears,
'Peck,' says the hen.

Q

What does Q stand for?
'Queen,' says the throne,
'Quiet,' says the librarian,
'Quarry,' says the stone,
The bed says 'Quilt,'
The arrow says 'Quiver,'
'Quack! Quack! Quack!'
Say the ducks on the river.

R

What does R stand for?
'Rails,' says the train,
'Rubbish,' says the bin,
The cloud says 'Rain,'
'Rhymes,' says the poet,
'Ruff,' says the dog,
'Rumble,' says the tummy,
'Ribbit,' says the frog.

S

What does S stand for?
'Secret,' says the spy,
The cards say 'Shuffle,'
The eagle says 'Sky,'
'Sleep,' says the pillow,
The winter says 'Snow,'
'Sizzle,' says the sausage,
The snail says 'Slow'.

T

What does T stand for?
'Twinkle,' says the star,
'Treasure,' says the pirate,
'Twang,' says the guitar,
The elephant says 'Tusk,'
'Twiddle,' says the thumb,
The storm says 'Thunder,'
'Tap-tap,' says the drum.

U

What does U stand for?
'Unfold,' says the map,
'Undo,' says the button.
The parcel says 'Unwrap,'
The ambulance says 'Urgent!'
'Underground,' says the mole,
The pale princess says 'Unicorn,'
'Ugly,' says the troll.

V

What does V stand for?
'Voyage,' says the crew,
'Valley,' says the river,
The window says 'View,'
Dracula says 'Vampire,'
'Vacant,' says the room,
The motorbike says, with a roar:
'Vroom! Vroom! Vroom!'

Vroom!
Vroom!

VACANT

W

What does W stand for?

'Wet,' says the ditch,

'Wake up!' says the alarm clock,

The wizard says 'Witch,'

The worm says 'Wriggle,'

'Water,' says the fish,

'Wash up,' say the dirty plates,

The genie says 'Wish'.

X

What does X stand for?
Not a lot at all,
'X-ray,' says the doctor,
When you've had a fall,
Xylophone and Xmas —
But that's only two,
Can't think of eXtra ones with X . . .
Can you?

Y

What does Y stand for?
'Yoghurt,' says the pot,
The sun says 'Yellow,'
The sailor says 'Yacht,'
'Yawn,' says the sleepyhead,
The dough says 'Yeast,'
'You,' says the mirror,
'Yeti,' says the beast.

Z

What does Z stand for?
'Zip,' says the pocket,
'Zapping,' says the remote control,
'Zoom,' says the rocket,
'Zombie,' says the nightmare,
The zebra says 'Zoo,'
'Zonked,' says me,
Having done these rhymes for you!

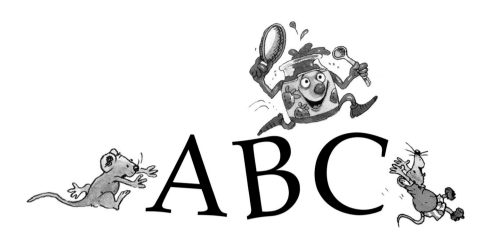

ABC

Aa

A, A, Annie Bly
Ate an alligator pie.

Bb

B, B, Baby Bear,
Bouncy-bouncing everywhere.

Cc

C, C, Clever Cilla
Caught a creepy caterpillar.

Dd

D, D, Doctor Daw,
Dancing with a dinosaur.

E, E, E_ggs on toast,
Edie Greedy eats the most.

F, F, F_armer Fred
Found a froggy in his bed.

I, I, I_cy nose,
Icy fingers, icy toes.

J, J, J_enni Kelly
Juggles jars of jam and jelly.

M, M, M_innie Moany
Married Mr Macaroni.

N, N, N_ick O'Shea
Nibbles noodles night and day.

G, G, Granny's cat
Got the giggles. Fancy that!

H, H, Hip hooray,
Hippo had a holiday.

K, K, King Canute
Keeps a kipper in his boot.

L, L, Little Molly
Likes to lick a lemon lolly.

O, O, One, two, three,
Octopuses chasing me!

P, P, Percy Parrot
Pecked a piece of pickled carrot.

Q, Q, Quiet please!
Queen Matilda's eating peas.

R, R, Rosie Farden
Rode a rabbit round the garden.

U, U, Uncle Joe
Underneath a drift of snow.

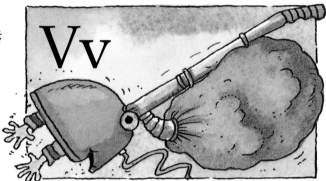

V, V, Vani Veena
Vanished in a vacuum cleaner.

Y, Y, Yum-yum-yum,
Yellow yoghurt for my tum.

Z, Z, Zoom and zip,
Zebra in a rocket ship.

Ss

S, S, Suki Soo
Sat upon a splinter. Ooo!

Tt

T, T, Teena Treen,
Training on a trampoline.

Ww

W, W, Willie worm,
Will he wiggle? Will he squirm?

Xx

X, X, Xixi Xee
Found a piXie up a tree.